T5-AFT-253

ISBN 0-8317-4915-6

Gallery Books are available for bulk purchase for
sales promotions and premium use. For details
write or telephone the Manager of Special Sales,
W. H. Smith Publishers, Inc., 112 Madison
Avenue, New York, NY 10016.
(212) 532 6600

Typeset by Best-Set Typesetter Ltd, Hong Kong
Printed and bound in Singapore

# CINDERELLA

## AND OTHER FAIRY TALES

### ILLUSTRATED BY RENE CLOKE

## GALLERY BOOKS
An Imprint of W. H. Smith Publishers Inc.

THEY WATCHED THE MEN QUARRELING

# CONTENTS

# CINDERELLA

ONCE there was a girl called Cinderella. She had two ugly step-sisters, who made her do all the house-work. While they wore fine dresses and slept in soft feather beds, Cinderella was dressed in rags and had to sleep in the cinders by the fire.

One day the King announced he was holding a ball for the Prince, who was looking for a bride. Every girl in the kingdom was invited. Cinderella's greedy stepsisters both decided to go.

"Wash my dress and iron my petticoat!"

"Polish my shoes and find my necklace!"
"Help me dress and do my hair!"
"Order the carriage! Fetch a pin!"
Their orders were endless, and poor
Cinderella had no time to do anything
for herself until it was too late.

"I wish I could go to the ball," sobbed

Cinderella after the sisters had left.

"Your wish will be granted," said a kind voice. A strange little old woman appeared, holding a magic wand. "I am your Fairy Godmother, and I have come to help you," she explained.

"But how can I go to the ball? I have nothing to wear except these old rags," protested Cinderella.

"Be patient and I will show you," her Fairy Godmother promised. "Now, do you have a pumpkin?" she asked.

Cinderella went into the garden in the moonlight and picked the best pumpkin she could find. With a wave of her magic wand the Fairy Godmother changed it into a shining golden coach.

After that she told Cinderella to find six mice, a rat and six lizards. The Fairy Godmother changed these into six horses, a coachman and six footmen. And then suddenly Cinderella found that she was no longer wearing rags but a beautiful gown and dainty glass slippers.

"Now off you go to the ball, my dear, and enjoy yourself," said the Fairy God-mother, "but remember one thing. You

"YOU SHALL GO TO THE BALL!"

must leave the palace by midnight or the spell will be broken.''

Cinderella thanked her Fairy God-mother and promised she would not forget. Then she stepped into the golden coach and rode off to the palace.

All the other guests had arrived. The Prince had seen hundreds of pretty girls but he could not decide which one should be his wife. The King could not even persuade him to dance with anyone.

Then Cinderella was announced. She looked so beautiful that all the guests at the ball stopped talking and turned to admire her.

As soon as the Prince saw Cinderella, he gave a deep bow and asked her to dance. He had fallen in love with her at first sight. They danced for hours, without a glance at anyone else. The King was pleased to see his son looking so happy. But Cinderella's stepsisters and some of the other guests were rather jealous.

"Who is that beautiful girl?" people asked. But nobody recognized her.

"That girl who has kept the Prince all to herself the whole evening reminds me of someone," one stepsister said to the

THE PRINCE ASKED HER TO DANCE

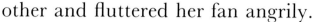

other and fluttered her fan angrily.

"Yes, I feel I know her too, but I cannot think who she is," her sister agreed.

The Prince and Cinderella danced on. The hands of the ballroom clock approached midnight, but she did not notice. Then the clock began to chime and she remembered her Fairy Godmother's warning.

"I must go!" Cinderella cried in alarm.

She dashed from the ballroom and fled down the steps of the palace. As she ran, one of her glass slippers flew off and was left behind.

"Wait! You must tell me your name," cried the Prince, but it was too late.

The Prince ordered his servants to search for her. One of them returned carrying the glass slipper. "Nobody saw any guest leave the palace, but this was

lying on the steps," the servant said.
The next day the Prince set out to find

CINDERELLA LOST A GLASS SLIPPER

the mysterious girl. His servants carried the glass slipper on a cushion.

"Every girl in the kingdom must try the slipper on. I will marry whichever one it fits," announced the Prince.

They visited one house after another, but not one girl had such dainty feet. When they came to Cinderella's home the ugly sisters tried in vain to cram their big feet into the slipper.

"May I try?" Cinderella asked shyly, appearing from the kitchen.

The slipper fitted her perfectly. Then Cinderella took out the other slipper and put it on too. Everyone was amazed.

At that moment Cinderella's Fairy Godmother appeared and tapped Cinderella with her magic wand. Cinderella's rags were instantly transformed into the magnificent gown she had worn at the ball. Then everyone recognized her.

"At last I have found you!" said the Prince joyfully. He took Cinderella in

IT FITTED HER TINY FOOT PERFECTLY

his arms and asked her to marry him.

The royal wedding took place a short while later. The bells all over the town rang out to announce the good news.

Cinderella, who was as kind as she was beautiful, forgave her stepsisters for the horrid way they had treated her. She even found noblemen for them to marry. And Cinderella and her Prince lived happily ever after at the palace.

"AT LAST I HAVE FOUND YOU!"

# TOM
# THUMB

THERE was once a man and his wife who had no children, although they both longed for a son or daughter.

"I do wish I had a baby, even if it were no bigger than my thumb," said the wife.

Then, at last, a child was born. It was a tiny baby boy and, strangely, however much he ate he never grew any bigger. Everybody called him Tom Thumb.

Tom made up for his small size by being the boldest and brightest of all the children in the village.

His father used to carry the little

fellow around safely in his pocket. But Tom was always looking for adventure and wanted to see the world.

"Let me ride in the brim of your hat, father," he asked. "Then I can whisper in your ear." So his father let him.

When Tom's mother went to milk the

cow she took him with her. He used to wander off and get lost while exploring the weeds that seemed like a jungle to him. Tom's mother was afraid she would not be able to find him, or that he would get trampled underfoot by the cow. He might even get blown away! So she tied him to the stem of a thistle with a wisp of hay. Unfortunately, the cow decided that Tom's thistle looked particularly tasty, and she bit it off. Tom only just managed to escape from her grinding teeth and jump to the ground, much to the cow's surprise.

But even after that Tom was not afraid of large animals. He wanted to join in everything and was full of clever ideas.

"Let me drive the horse and cart, father," he begged, when his father needed to fetch wood one day. "I'll sit in the horse's ear and give directions."

Tom's father agreed to let him help. People were astonished to see the cart being pulled along by a horse that

THE COW WAS AS SURPRISED AS TOM WAS

seemed to have no rider in the saddle.

When Tom was not sitting in the horse's ear, he liked to stand and shout at the horse, cracking a whip. This was no ordinary whip, but a special one his father had made him out of a stalk of barley. One day, a huge black raven suddenly swooped down. It picked up Tom's barley-stalk whip with Tom still clinging to it. The bird flew up into a tree, where it was building a nest.

It took Tom a very long time to climb out of the nest. When he looked down at the ground he realized it would be too difficult to climb down.

However, one branch of the tree hung over the river, and brave Tom decided to risk getting wet! He crawled along to the end of the branch and was about to dive into the water.

Just then a giant came along the river-bank. Although he was very tall, his eyesight was poor. He was also greedy. Thinking Tom was a new kind of berry, the giant picked him off the twig. Then

TOM WAS STILL CLINGING TO THE STALK

he popped him into his mouth and swallowed him whole.

Tom was furious to find himself trapped in the giant's dark stomach, and he began to kick and shout. The giant heard his tummy rumbling. He felt some uncomfortable, sharp, stabbing pains. His tummy ache was caused by Tom's boots!

Finally, the giant gave a cough, and Tom shot out of his mouth and landed in the river. He started swimming for the bank. But before he reached land, a big fish saw him and gobbled him up.

That might have been the end of Tom if the fish had not been caught by a fisherman only a few minutes later. The fish was an extra-large one, and it ended up in the palace kitchen to be cooked and served to the King himself.

The cook got an awful shock when he

THE GIANT HAD A PAIN IN HIS TUMMY

cut the fish open and out popped Tom Thumb.

"How ever did you get in there?" he asked in surprise. So Tom began to tell him all his adventures.

The cook was so fascinated that he sat listening for hours. Then suddenly he realized he had forgotten to cook the King's and Queen's dinner.

"Oh, my goodness, whatever shall I do? I will lose my job for certain," wailed the worried cook.

Tom had always been a bold, clever lad with a knack for talking his way out of any trouble. "Leave it to me," he assured the cook. "Just do exactly as I say and everything will be all right, I promise you."

"Send a message to the King," Tom ordered. "Tell him to expect a surprise for dinner. I shall entertain him as he has never been entertained before. Make sure that the musicians are ready with their instruments, for we shall be wanting some music. Now take me in to meet the King," said Tom. "I'd like to be

HE GAVE THE COOK QUITE A SHOCK

carried in on a large silver plate."

The cook felt very uneasy. "What a nerve this little fellow Tom Thumb has," he thought to himself.

But the cook obeyed, although his knees were knocking with fear as he hurried along the corridor.

Tom was not the least bit afraid. He danced and twirled and admired his reflection in the silver plate.

The cook need not have worried, for the King was in a very good mood that day. He roared with laughter when the cook brought in the tiny figure twirling happily on the silver plate.

"When you said I should expect a surprise for dinner, I thought I was going to eat it, not meet it," the King chuckled. "Where did this little morsel come from?" he asked, picking Tom up gently.

TOM PREPARED TO MEET THE KING

When the cook told him the story about Tom popping out of the fish, he was even more amused.

The King set Tom down on the table and asked. "What have you got to say for yourself, little man?"

Tom gave a low bow and began to tell his tale. The King and all the men from the court listened to the story of Tom's amazing adventures.

When the Queen saw Tom she liked him so much that she asked the King to invite him to stay at the palace as their special guest.

"With pleasure, Your Majesties," Tom agreed. "But first I must visit my own father and mother to tell them I am safe and well."

Now that he was a member of the royal court, Tom was given a fine suit of

THE KING WAS GREATLY AMUSED

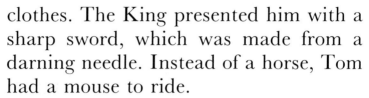

clothes. The King presented him with a sharp sword, which was made from a darning needle. Instead of a horse, Tom had a mouse to ride.

The whole court assembled to see him go, and Tom Thumb rode home in triumph astride his trusty white mouse.

His mother and father were overjoyed to see their tiny son once more, as they had feared him dead. Pretty soon, Tom had persuaded them to come and live with him at the palace so that they could all be together. They all lived happily ever after.

TOM BECAME A MEMBER OF THE COURT

# BABES
# IN
# THE WOOD

THERE were once two little children who lived with an old uncle. Their rich father had left them a lot of money when he died. While they were still young, their uncle looked after the money for them.

At first their uncle treated them well, but then he decided he wanted all the money for himself. So he sent for two wicked men he knew and offered them a bag of gold if they would pretend to kidnap the children and take them away.

The next morning the children were

HE SENT FOR TWO WICKED MEN

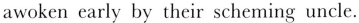

awoken early by their scheming uncle.

"Get up quickly. I have arranged a special treat for you. Two friends of mine will take you for a picnic in the woods," he told them.

The men, who were really robbers, took the two children for a long walk in the forest. One of the men was very kind to them, for he really loved children. But the other robber was rather rough, for he was greedy for the gold.

After they had gone several miles the children grew tired. The kind robber gave the little girl a ride on his shoulder, but the fierce robber dragged the boy along by the arm.

"Hurry up!" he grumbled.

They went deeper into the forest, where the bushes and brambles grew thick and thorny beneath the tall trees.

THEY HURRIED THROUGH THE WOODS

Finally, they stopped in a clearing.

"We have gone far enough," said the fierce robber, and he grabbed Tom roughly again.

The children realized then that these were wicked men, and they started to cry. The kind robber did not like to see them frightened, and he tried to stop his partner from being so rough.

The two men started to quarrel. They drew their swords and began to fight. Finally the kind robber won.

Quickly he took both children and hurried away with them, going even deeper into the forest.

The robber knew he must escape before anyone discovered what had happened. He left the children while he tried to find the way out of the woods, but then he could not find his way back to them.

The children wandered along alone, feeling very tired and hungry. The boy tried calling for help, but there was nobody to hear. His sister started to cry. They sat down to rest on a mossy

THE ROBBERS BEGAN TO FIGHT

bank, and some of the little forest animals gathered around them. A squirrel scampered up and dropped a few nuts. Then a little bird fluttered by with a juicy berry.

AT FIRST THEY WERE FRIGHTENED

The children followed it and found a whole bush of berries to pick and eat. A pretty fawn led them to a clear pool where they could drink.

All the small animals in the forest helped to care for them. The children were delighted to make friends. They stroked the furry creatures, and the birds ate from their hands.

The days went by and the children lived safely and happily in the forest among the animals and birds. They stopped feeling sad and frightened.

A short time later, the children's uncle died. People wondered what had become of the children who had lived with him.

Then the robber was captured. He confessed to all his crimes and told his guards how he had left the two children all alone in the woods.

Some people went into the forest to look for the children. After a long search they found the two children fast asleep on a mossy bank under the trees. The birds had kept them warm by covering them with a blanket of leaves.

Everyone was pleased that the children were safe and sound. Kind friends gave them a new home, and from that day on the two children were known as the Babes in the Wood.

THE ANIMALS LOOKED AFTER THEM